BEWARE
OF GIRLS

Tony Blundell

PUFFIN BOOKS

*For Christopher Bullard
and Katherine Scott,
who write very good stories!*

PUFFIN BOOKS

Published by the Penguin Group
Penguin Books Ltd, 80 Strand, London WC2R 0RL, England
Penguin Group (USA), Inc., 375 Hudson Street, New York, New York 10014, USA
Penguin Books Australia Ltd, 250 Camberwell Road, Camberwell, Victoria 3124, Australia
Penguin Books Canada Ltd, 10 Alcorn Avenue, Toronto, Ontario, Canada M4V 3B2
Penguin Books India (P) Ltd, 11 Community Centre, Panchsheel Park, New Delhi – 110 017, India
Penguin Group (NZ), cnr Airborne and Rosedale Roads, Albany, Auckland 1310, New Zealand
Penguin Books (South Africa) (Pty) Ltd, 24 Sturdee Avenue, Rosebank 2196, South Africa

www.penguin.com

Penguin Books Ltd, Registered Offices: 80 Strand, London WC2R 0RL, England

First published 2002
9 10

Copyright © Tony Blundell, 2002
All rights reserved

The moral right of the author/illustrator has been asserted

Set in Sabon 17/22pt

Manufactured in China

British Library Cataloguing in Publication Data
A CIP catalogue record for this book is available from the British Library

ISBN-13: 978-0-14056-660-4

Once upon a dark, damp evening deep in the forest, a hungry wolf sat in his cave reading a book about little girls and grandmas.

The wolf was not very good at reading, but the pictures made him feel very hungry indeed!

And they gave the wolf a brilliant idea!

So, the very next morning, the inspired wolf trotted down the path out of the forest and knocked upon the door of a little girl's cottage.

The little girl opened the door just a crack and looked the wolf up and down.

"Hello, little girl," said the wolf. "I'm your grandma and I've come for my breakfast – may I come in?"

The little girl's dog started barking, "WOLF–WOLF–WOLF!!"

"Be quiet, Rexy," she said.

Then she gave the wolf her long, thoughtful look and said, "I really don't think you can be my grandma, because my grandma always wears a big, pretty, flowery dress and she always brings me a big basket of newly laid eggs and a jar of runny honey and a warm crusty loaf for my breakfast!"

And saying that, she shut the door in the wolf's face.

"Oh, does she!" said the wolf, and then quickly changed it to: "Oh, do I!" And he raced off up the road to see what he could do about it.

When the wolf got back to his cave, he rummaged through all his boxes and trunks . . .

. . . till he found a big, pretty, flowery dress, which used to belong to his grandma . . .

. . . and he wriggled himself into it!

Then he visited the beehives . . .

. . . and the chicken huts . . .

. . . and the baker's!

Soon the wolf was back again, knocking at the cottage door.

"Hello, little girl," he said. "I'm your grandma in a big, pretty, flowery dress, with a basket of newly laid honey and a jar of eggs and a warm runny loaf, and I've come for my lunch – may I come in?"

The little girl took the basket and sniffed the warm bread hungrily.

Her little dog was jumping up and down and barking, "WOLF–WOLF–WOLF!!"

"Oh, Rexy, do be quiet," said the little girl.

Then she gave the wolf her long, thoughtful look and she said, "I really don't think you can be my grandma, because she always wears a big feathery hat and she always brings me a big bowl of yummy trifle for my pudding!"

And saying that, she shut the door in the wolf's face.

"So I do!" said the wolf, who was beginning to get the hang of this game. And he raced off up the road to see what he could do about it.

When the wolf got back to his cave, he burst open all the cushions and pillows . . .

. . . till he had enough feathers to make a big, floppy, feathery hat.

Then he got out the
food mixer . . .

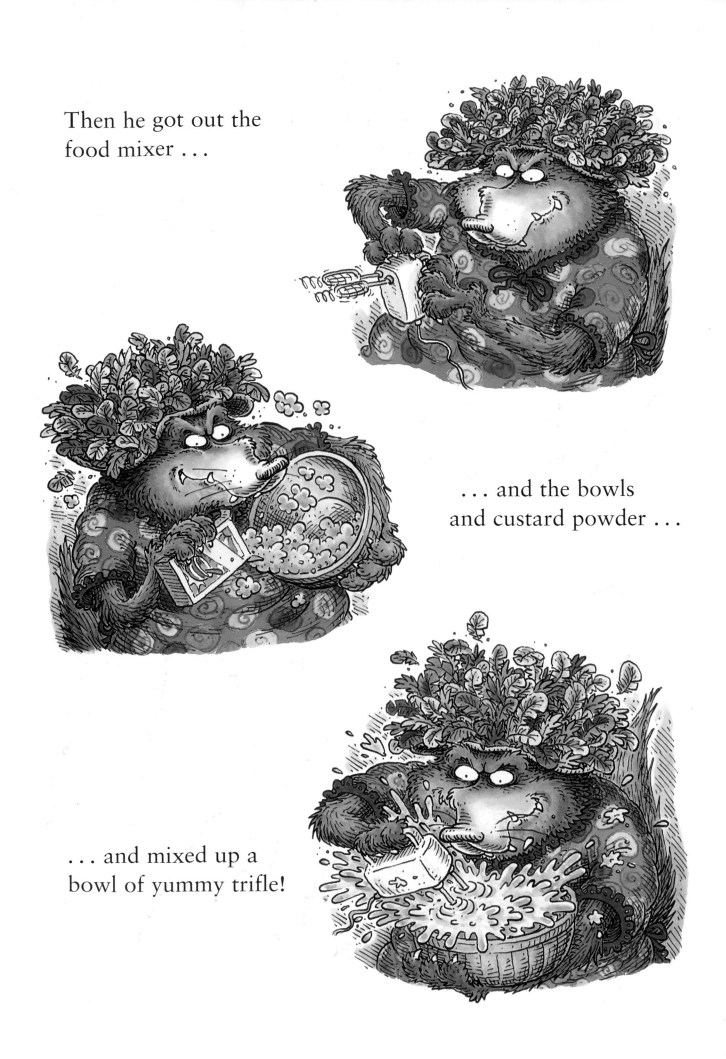

. . . and the bowls
and custard powder . . .

. . . and mixed up a
bowl of yummy trifle!

It was not long before the wolf was once again knocking on the cottage door.

"Hello, little girl," said the wolf. "I'm your grandma in her big feathery dress, with a yummy flowery hat and a pretty bowl of trifle and I've come for my tea – may I come in?"

The little girl took the bowl of trifle and dipped her finger in it. "Mmm," she said, "yummy!"

Rexy was going potty. "WOLF–WOLF–WOLF–WOLF–WOOLFF!!" he barked.

"Rexy, don't be so silly," said the little girl.

And once again she gave the wolf her long, thoughtful look and she said, "I really don't think you can be my grandma, because she always wears bright-red high-heeled shoes and she always brings me a bag of sticky toffee and a great big chocolate cake for my tea . . . oh, and some doggy-treats for Rexy!" she added.

And saying that, she shut the door in the wolf's face again.

"Oh yes, I must have forgotten," growled the wolf through gritted teeth, and he set off again to see what he could do about it.

When the wolf got back to his cave, he searched through
all his old trunks and boxes . . .

. . . till he found a pair of his grandma's high-heeled shoes . . .

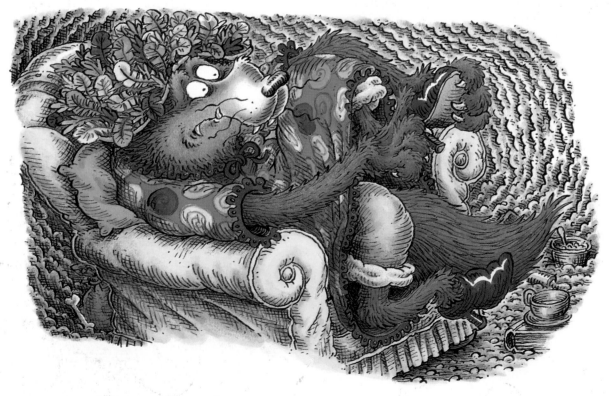

. . . which he wriggled his feet into.

Then he made some
sticky toffee ...

... and a great big
chocolate cake ...

... and he didn't forget
the doggy-treats!

So it was a rather tired and sticky wolf who came knocking once again on the cottage door.

"Hello, little girl," said the wolf. "I am your grandma in her big sticky dress and her bright-red hat and her pretty chocolate shoes, with a bag of feathery toffees and a great big high-heeled cake, and I've come for my supper – may I come in?"

"WOLF–WOLF–WOLF–WOLF–WOLF–WOLF–WOLF–
WOLFF!!" shouted Rexy.

"And some doggy-treats for Rexy?" asked the little girl.

"Oh yes, of course!" growled the wolf, and handed them over. "Now can I come in?"

"Well," said the little girl, giving the wolf her long, thoughtful look, "I still don't think you can be my grandma, because my grandma always carries a very large rock around with her, and she always has a big bunch of balloons tied to her tail!"

And saying that, she shut the door in the wolf's face.

"Some grandmas are very strange," grumbled the wolf as he tottered back up the road in his high-heels.

"Grandma or not," he growled, "the next time I knock on that door, it's supper-time for me!"

When the wolf got back to the forest, he found the
biggest rock that he could possibly carry ...

... then he staggered into town and found a balloon-seller ...

... and tied all the balloons to his tail.

It was quite some time later that one very weary wolf came knocking on the cottage door, a large rock clasped in his arms and a big bunch of balloons tied to his tail.

"Hello, little girl," he gasped. "I'm your grandma, and –"

"Why, hello, Grandma, how very nice to see you!" said the little girl. "Do come inside and have a bite to eat."

"Brilliant!" gasped the wolf.

"Oh, but before you do, Grandma, do put that big rock down – it looks so very heavy!"

So the wolf let go of the rock.

And, as soon as he did so, the big bunch of balloons tied to his tail lifted him majestically up into the sky.

"Going so soon, Grandma?" said the little girl. "What a shame!" And she went inside to enjoy her tea of bread and honey, chocolate cake and yummy trifle.

Up and up went the wolf.

Up above the trees.

Up above the forest.

Up and up, until he was just a tiny dot in the sky!

And even now, sometimes on a clear night, a strange shape crosses the moon and if you are very quiet you may hear the distant sound of grinding teeth, and the rumbling of one very empty tummy!

The End.